RII

June Crebbin was ....y school teacher before taking early retirement to concentrate on her writing. She is the author of a number of books for children, including the first two stories about Merryfield Hall Riding School, *Jumping Beany* and *Saving Oscar*, as well as several picture books for younger children. June lives in Leicestershire, where she enjoys riding in the countryside and in the dressage arena.

More books about
Merryfield Hall Riding School

Jumping Beany
Saving Oscar

More books by the same author

The Curse of the Skull
The Dragon Test
Emmelina and the Monster
Hal the Highwayman
Horse Tales
No Tights for George!
Tarquin the Wonder Horse

Riding High

June Crebbin

WALKER
BOOKS

First published 2008 by Walker Books Ltd
87 Vauxhall Walk, London SE11 5HJ

2 4 6 8 10 9 7 5 3 1

Text © 2008 June Crebbin
Cover photograph © Wayne Hutchinson/Alamy

The right of June Crebbin to be identified as author
of this work has been asserted by her in accordance
with the Copyright, Designs and Patents Act 1988

This book has been typeset in Stempel Schneidler

Printed and bound in Great Britain by
Clays Ltd, St Ives plc

British Library Cataloguing in Publication Data:
a catalogue record for this book
is available from the British Library

ISBN 978-1-4063-1123-5

www.walker.co.uk

For Isabella, Amelia, Georgia,
Hugo and Lucy

With special thanks to Gail and Mel

Amber ran down the lane, keeping a firm hold of the two ponies she was leading. The children riding them shrieked with delight. This was their treat, a trot up the lane and back at the end of the lesson.

Keep going, Amber willed Kate, the riding instructor running in front of her. But Kate was slowing her ponies to a walk and Amber had to do the same.

Amber loved being a helper at Merryfield Hall Riding School, especially on Saturdays when she looked after the little ones, showing them how to tack and untack their ponies and putting up jumps.

But today, Kate's lessons were running late and over the hedge Amber could already see the other helpers riding into the outside arena for their free lesson. Amber couldn't wait to join them with Oscar, the pony she was lucky enough to have on loan. She exercised Oscar every day but the only lessons she had at the moment were free ones. Money had been in short supply ever since Dad had his accident.

Kate turned into the yard. "You'll untack for me, won't you?" she called.

"But I have to get Oscar!" cried Amber.

"It won't take long," said Kate.

"Thanks a lot," muttered Amber. She helped her riders dismount. One little boy had brought carrots but he kept dropping them before the pony could eat them.

"Shall I help?" said Amber.

"No," said the boy. "I can do it."

Amber's best friend, Molly, passed by on Feather.

"Are you coming?" she said. "Our lesson's starting."

"I know," said Amber, as she rescued yet another piece of carrot from the ground. "But first I've got to finish up here and then go and get Oscar and…"

But when she looked up, Molly had gone.

At last the boy let Amber put her hand under his. "That's it!" she said. "Keep your fingers flat. Brilliant!"

The boy beamed.

"See you next week," said Amber.

She hurried the ponies into their stalls, untacked, put everything away, and took Oscar to the outside arena. "Can I come in?" she called.

"Join the end of the ride," said Mel, who was taking the lesson. "We're doing spirals."

Amber concentrated. Each rider in turn rode their pony in ever decreasing circles to the centre of the arena and then spiralled out again.

"Inside leg as you come out!" shouted Mel. "Don't rely on your reins."

By the third attempt Amber and Oscar had got the hang of it. Easy to go inwards, thought Amber, outside leg and softer inside rein. But much harder to push Oscar out. She could see how it helped their balance though.

They did the same exercise again at the trot and somehow that seemed easier. Maybe because they'd practised at walk first. Then they cantered on each rein. But not in spirals!

"Who wants to jump?" said Mel.

Everyone yelled approval, except Molly who was a bit scared of jumping.

Oscar enjoyed himself. Amber had been working really hard with him on his turns and he was getting much steadier. It was all very well flying round a course but sometimes Oscar was so eager, Amber found it difficult to line him up for the next jump.

After the lesson, Amber went to the office. Molly was reading a notice: TRAIL RIDING IN THE WELSH MOUNTAINS.

"What's trail riding?" she said.

"You know, pony-trekking," said Amber. It sounded exciting.

"I think you'd both enjoy it," said Jen, the owner of Merryfield Hall Riding School, looking up from the computer. "You're certainly capable."

Amber read the notice. Three days riding in Wales, the first night staying at a hill farm, the second night – wild camping!

"No amenities there!" said Jen. "You'd be riding miles from anywhere. Just a river or stream for washing in."

"Fantastic!" said Amber.

"Would there be any jumping?" said Molly.

Jen laughed. "Not unless you count the odd ditch!" she said. "You'd be travelling long distances so it's mainly walk and trot."

"And canters," added Amber. "It says 'canters on grassy tracks'."

"On the second day you carry all your equipment with you," said Jen. "My friend Lisa, who runs it, says it would be good preparation if you wanted to take part in an award scheme when you're older."

Amber had read about those in one of her pony books. Finding your way on horseback from one place to another; map reading; looking after your pony; all without an escort. It sounded a real challenge.

"Look," said Jen, "I've had some leaflets printed. Why don't you take one home and have a think about it? But don't be too long. It'll get booked up pretty quickly."

While Amber and Molly waited for Molly's mum to pick them up, they read the leaflets in detail.

"An escort goes with us this time," said Molly. "Thank goodness."

"It says you can take your own pony!"

said Amber. Imagine riding Oscar not just for an hour's hack but all day for miles and miles.

"Oh, if only I could take Feather," said Molly.

Molly always rode Feather but he was a school horse.

"Listen to this," said Amber. "'All our ponies are friendly, love being groomed and are easy to tack up.' And," she read on, "'they wait at the gate in the morning eager for another day in the hills.' You'd be fine."

By the time Molly's mum arrived, Molly was as enthusiastic as Amber.

"Three whole days," she said as they drove off, "and I'd be completely in charge of my own pony!"

"Riding high in the mountains," added Amber.

"With wild camping," said Molly.

Molly's mum smiled. "How much?" she said.

Molly checked the leaflet. "Only two hundred and fifty pounds," she said.

Amber's heart sank. She hadn't given a thought to how much it would cost. How stupid! How could there possibly be money for expeditions when there was none for lessons?

"Only!" exclaimed Molly's mum.

"But you're always wanting me to try new things," wheedled Molly.

Amber was quiet for the rest of the journey home. When they reached her gate she said goodbye and walked slowly up the path. Her parents had been so pleased for her when Emma, Oscar's owner, had asked Amber to look after her pony. Emma lived in Austria with her mum who paid all Oscar's expenses which was just as well since Dad had been off work so long. It takes time for two broken legs, seven cracked ribs and a dislocated shoulder to heal. Yet Dad loved his job as a stuntman!

Amber knew Gran was helping to pay for her sister Lily's dancing lessons. They weren't nearly as much as riding lessons. But maybe … just maybe Gran would help with trail riding! Even as she thought it, Amber dismissed the idea. She knew she couldn't ask Gran for that much money.

Amber let herself in at the back door. Slowly and carefully, she tore the leaflet into tiny pieces and stuffed them in the bin.

Over the next few days, Amber couldn't stop thinking about the trail riding trip. That was, how could she get enough cash to pay for it? There must be a way. It was a huge pity money didn't grow on trees, as in all the best fairy stories, or fall out of the sky. But in the real world, as Mum was fond of telling her, you had to work for it.

That's it! she thought. I work at the stables! Suppose Jen paid her instead of giving her a free lesson? Mel got paid. Amber had no idea how much but if it was ten pounds a week, say, it would soon add up. Though it would take twenty-five weeks to save up two hundred and fifty pounds. And there were only five weeks to go before the trip. She decided to ask Mel anyway. It might be more than she thought.

"You're too young," said Mel when Amber asked her. "You can't be paid until you're older."

So that was that.

What about a paper round? But after school she went straight to the stables. Then there was homework. She'd never fit it in.

Washing cars? But it was so easy to nip into a car wash. Although, come to think of it, none of the vehicles at the stables looked as if they'd ever been in one. That's it! thought Amber. She could set up a clean car centre in the corner of the riding school. She'd seen it done in town. You parked your car in the multi-storey, then while you were shopping, someone washed it. Perfect! Parents would arrive, go off to watch their children ride and return to a sparkling four by four or whatever.

Amber worked it out. She was at the stables by eight o'clock every Saturday. If she did one car an hour, giving her time to do her stable jobs as well, and charged two pounds, which was really cheap, and worked until five o'clock, that would be nine hours, making a total of eighteen pounds. And five weeks times eighteen pounds would be … well, nearly a hundred pounds.

Amber's excitement faded. Not enough. Not even half.

If there'd been more time … but she needed the money now. Even if she'd had a rich uncle, he'd have to die at once in order to leave her his millions.

It didn't help that Molly kept sending her ecstatic texts: "Mum sez I can go. Isn't it gr8?"

Amber didn't reply. It was just as well she and Molly went to different schools so she didn't have to answer in person.

After school on Wednesday, Amber was busy sweeping up when Donna arrived on her pony, Sparkle. Donna kept Sparkle at the livery stables at nearby Merryfield Hall. Amber saw them coming and kept her head down but Donna rode right up to her. "Hiya!" she greeted.

Amber looked up briefly and carried on wielding the broom.

"Just come for my lesson," trilled Donna. "Are you joining us today?"

Amber groaned. Donna knew perfectly well that Amber hadn't been to their usual lesson for months. She was probably aware of the reason why but she always insisted on asking. Amber braced herself for the next remark. Sure enough…

"What a shame you can't come," said Donna.

Molly arrived. "Why haven't you answered my texts?" she demanded.

"Sorry," said Amber.

She moved away but Molly followed. "Well, are you going or not?"

"Going where?" said Donna.

Molly and Amber looked up.

"Nowhere," they both said.

"Must be somewhere," said Donna. "You probably mean the trail riding weekend. Of course," she added, as she rode off, "Sparkle and I are going."

Molly and Amber exchanged horrified glances.

"I'll have to go," said Molly.

"Go where?" trilled Amber.

Molly giggled. "To my lesson, idiot!"

"Feather's all ready for you," said Amber.

"Thanks," said Molly. "See you later."

But Amber made sure she went home before the lesson finished. She knew how Molly would react when she explained that she couldn't go trail riding; she'd be really kind and say how sorry she was and she hadn't realized … and when all that was over Molly would still be going and Amber wouldn't.

That evening Amber was upstairs in her bedroom when the phone rang. If it's Molly, she thought, I'm out. She heard Mum answer. The voices went on for quite a while. Obviously not Molly then. Must be one of Mum's friends. It was a long conversation.

Eventually the voices stopped and Mum went back into the living room.

Amber decided to forget homework for the time being and check out her favourite website: www.luvURpony.com. She scrolled through the pages and paused at the Star Pony Keyring. It said, "This crimson plush pony is just the thing for keeping your keys safe. He comes with diamond-studded hooves and twinkling stars in his mane and tail. Or, if you don't want to use him as a keyring, you can simply 'pony-up' your schoolbag and be the envy of all your friends".

Amber sighed. He was so cute. For Oscar she would choose the Funky Spotted Travel Boots and Rug to Match.

"Amber!" It was Dad calling softly up the stairs. Amber knew he wouldn't want to wake Lily and her baby brother, Sam. And Dad wouldn't come up. He still found climbing the stairs difficult. She went to her bedroom door.

"Can you come and talk to us?" said Dad. "It won't take a minute."

Downstairs the living room was un-usually quiet. The television had been switched off. Amber looked at her parents. Dad was smiling but Mum kept shifting her position on the sofa. She seemed edgy.

"Have I done something?" asked Amber. She couldn't think what.

"Not as far as we know," said Dad. "But we were just wondering if you knew any-thing about a trail riding expedition in the Welsh mountains?"

Amber's thoughts raced. So it *had* been Molly on the phone, ringing up to speak to her and then rabbiting on to Mum.

"Molly shouldn't have told you!" Amber burst out. "I don't want to go anyway. It'll probably be boring, boring, boring. I'm not interested."

"Hang on," said Dad. "For a start, it wasn't Molly on the phone."

"Oh," said Amber.

"It was Donna—" started Mum.

"Donna?" Amber almost screamed.

"Donna's mother," continued Mum. "She was offering to pay for you."

Amber was shocked into silence. Why would Donna's mother want to pay for her? It wasn't as though she and Donna were friends. Far from it. But her heart leapt at the thought of going. Even with Donna. She couldn't help herself.

"Well, it's very kind of Donna's mother—" began Amber.

"*Kind?*" exploded Mum. "Kind doesn't come into it. Downright cheek in my opinion, implying that we can't afford it and playing the Lady Bountiful!"

"I'm sure she wasn't that bad," said Dad.

"You didn't have to listen," blazed Mum. "Anyway, I'm not having it."

Amber's hopes vanished.

"Let's all calm down," said Dad, though, actually, thought Amber, it was only Mum getting herself in a state, "and hear what Amber has to say."

Amber took a deep breath and told her parents all the details she could remember about the expedition and how she hadn't shown them the leaflet because she knew she couldn't afford to go.

"Do you want to?" asked Dad.

Amber nodded.

"Why?"

Amber was used to Dad's questioning. Whenever she wanted to do anything new,

Dad always asked her for reasons. Usually, Amber worked out her strategies very carefully before she approached him. On this occasion there'd been no time. But she didn't need it.

"Because," said Amber, "it's something I've never done before…"

"But you ride every day!" exclaimed Mum. "Why do you always want more?"

"Now that's not fair," said Dad. "Amber didn't even tell us about it until we asked." He turned to Amber. "Your mum's upset. It's not been easy for her this past year, taking on more and more dressmaking work and coping with me as well as Sam and you girls."

Amber stood up. "I'll go and finish my homework now, then, shall I?"

"No," said Mum. "If anyone's going to pay for my daughter to go anywhere, it'll be me."

Amber stared.

"I've got some savings," said Mum. "If you want to go, you can."

"But—" began Amber.

"No buts," interrupted Dad. "If your mother's made up her mind, no one in this world is going to change it."

Amber took the hint. She sprang across the room and threw her arms around Mum's neck. "If you're sure…?" she said. "I don't know how to thank you."

"Better get your name down tomorrow," said Mum.

"And bring us all the information," added Dad, "so we can see exactly what's involved."

Amber promised. She couldn't wait to tell Molly.

"Donna's mother also offered transport," said Mum. "For you and Oscar. Apparently their trailer is big enough for two ponies, but—"

"That," said Dad, "we can definitely accept. How very kind!"

The following day, Jen added Amber's name to the list. She seemed disappointed. "Only three of you," she said. "I thought there'd be lots more wanting to go but it appears everyone else has already made plans for half term."

"Is three enough?" asked Amber. "Will the trip be on?"

"Oh, yes," said Jen. "There's sure to be riders from other centres."

Molly was ecstatic when Amber phoned. "I didn't dare tell you before," said Molly, "but guess what? I'm travelling with Donna as well. It's so kind of her mum, isn't it?"

Amber had to agree. She couldn't believe that not only was she going, but Oscar was too! She made up her mind to be as nice and friendly as she possibly could to Donna. It was bound to be difficult considering most of the time she just wanted to hit her. But it would be Amber's way of thanking Donna's mum. If she hadn't phoned…

"I didn't realize you and Donna were friends," said Mum that evening as they were tidying up the kitchen after dinner.

"We're not," said Amber.

"Her mother spoke as if you were," said Mum. "She specifically mentioned how thrilled Donna would be to have her best friend along."

Amber shrugged. "Donna hasn't got any friends," she said. "She's so bossy and she's always going on about how amazing Sparkle is. It puts people off."

"I see," said Mum. "Won't that cause problems?"

"Don't worry," said Amber. "I'm going to be an angel!"

Dad came into the kitchen. "An angel? You?"

Amber grinned. "It's only for three days. I can manage that!" She hugged her mum. "I still can't believe I'm going!"

"Speaking of which," said Dad. "I've prepared a little activity for you."

Amber groaned. Dad's "little activities" usually turned out to be really long, time-consuming ones. But he had implied it was connected to the expedition. "What is it?" she asked.

"Map reading," said Dad.

"But the escort does all that kind of thing," said Amber. "We just ride."

"Nevertheless," said Dad. "It's a useful skill. You never know when you might need it."

On the living room table, Dad had spread out an Ordnance Survey map of part of

Wales. He explained how the scale meant everything was in much more detail than on the road map they used in the car. "So you can find locations of farms, churches, footpaths, hills, rivers, railways..."

"And bridleways!" said Amber, looking at the key at the side. "A line of dashes."

She scoured the map. "There don't seem to be many," she said.

"That's because you'll be in the mountains," said Dad. "I think you're more likely to travel along the old drovers' roads. The Welsh farmers used to drive their sheep to London along those routes."

"I can't wait!" said Amber.

"Now," said Dad. "Suppose you've stopped for lunch and you need to check in at base. You want to tell them exactly where you are—"

"I won't," said Amber. "I told you. Jen said we don't need to know any of that stuff yet. She said the main purpose of this expedition was to get used to riding long distances in a different terrain."

"I'll just tell you a bit," said Dad. "It won't take long."

Amber resisted the impulse to say she'd heard that before. Dad looked so eager. "OK then," she said. "But I do have homework."

To her surprise, Amber found she enjoyed working out the six-digit grid references Dad gave her, pinpointing a junction or a bridge or a bend in the river. Then she gave Dad references to solve.

"You've done really well," said Dad, as they packed the map away. "I think your next challenge will be—" he paused dramatically— "survival!"

"Like how to tackle a tiger single-handed, I suppose," said Amber. "Or sail down a crocodile-infested river on a log. Dad, I'm not riding deep in the jungle, just high in the hills!"

31

* * *

In the weeks that followed, it seemed to Amber that the day of departure would never arrive. When it did, she woke to the sound of heavy rain clattering against the windows. But nothing was going to dampen her spirits today of all days.

"Rain before seven, dry before eleven," she sang to herself as she dressed.

Everything was ready. Donna's mother would call for Molly, then pick up Sparkle and last of all collect Amber and Oscar from the riding school.

Amber skipped through the puddles in the stable yard as she went backwards and forwards, fetching things for Oscar's journey. Jen had lent him some proper travelling boots. Admittedly, they were bright blue and didn't really go with his sunshine yellow rug but never mind, Amber told herself, they would protect his legs; that was what mattered. Though if Sparkle turned up with Funky Spotted Boots and a Rug to Match, Amber would explode. No she wouldn't, she suddenly remembered. She would just say, "How lovely Sparkle looks!" Or something.

At last Oscar was ready. Eight o'clock. The rain had stopped. The trailer should arrive any time now. Amber went out to the gate to watch for it.

Steam rose from the ground as the day warmed up. It was going to be fine, Amber thought. She saw Donna's car turn the corner at the end of the lane.

They were coming!

It was only when they drove in through the gateway that Amber realized it was just the car. There was no pony-trailer.

"What's happened?" she cried, as Donna got out of the car. "Where's Sparkle?"

Jen came out to speak to Donna's mother.

"He's gone lame," said Donna.

"Oh," said Amber. "I'm so sorry. Will he be all right?"

"He just needs rest," grumbled Donna. "It would have to happen now."

"But where's the trailer?" said Amber. She felt genuinely sorry for Donna and Sparkle but surely that didn't affect the travel arrangements.

"No point bringing the trailer for just one pony, is there?" snapped Donna.

She turned away, reaching for the door handle of the car.

Something in Amber's head burst. She leapt forward and grabbed Donna's shoulder.

"You mean, because Sparkle can't go, Oscar can't either?"

Donna shook her off.

"Are you ready?" she shouted to her mother. She wrenched the car door open. "Shall we go?"

The journey to Wales was not a comfortable one. Amber sank into the
thick, padded leather seats well enough.
But the atmosphere was tense. At first
Donna's mother attempted to make jolly
conversation but Molly was the only one
who joined in. Donna sat in tight-lipped
silence. Amber stared out of the win-
dow, trying not to let the tears pricking at
the back of her eyelids overflow. Jen had
assured her before they'd left that she
would look after Oscar. It wouldn't be a
problem. She'd urged all of them to enjoy
riding different ponies. "They're used to

travelling in the hills," she'd told them. "It'll be fun!"

But Amber had so looked forward to enjoying the trip with Oscar. She tried to tell herself she was lucky to be going. After all, that had seemed impossible five weeks ago. But they could easily have brought Oscar. It was so unfair.

They reached the trail centre in a couple of hours. Amber was relieved to be out of the car. Lisa was waiting to greet them. Then it was all hustle and bustle sorting out luggage and packing lunches into panniers along with other necessities until Donna's mother said goodbye. Amber remembered to thank her.

"Now for your ponies!" said Lisa. "Jen rang me to say you'd all need mounts. So come and meet them."

The girls followed her to a courtyard. Four ponies were tied up at one side, busily eating. They looked up briefly as the girls approached, then went back to their munching.

Amber wondered which pony would be hers. They all looked strong and hardworking.

Lisa introduced them. "Molly, this is Clover. He's the quietest of all our ponies. I think you'll like him."

"Oh, I will," said Molly, beaming, as she reached forward to pat the stocky red roan.

"And this is Gus," said Lisa, moving on to a thick-set, sturdy skewbald with a long straggly mane and feathers at his heels. "He's your mount, Donna."

Donna stared in disbelief. "I'm not riding him," she said. "He looks like a carthorse."

Lisa smiled. "He's really very sweet," she said, "and very comfortable." She moved on. "And you'll be riding High Jinks, Amber. Now don't get the wrong idea. He doesn't live up to his name. He's forward going but he doesn't lark about!"

High Jinks looked up as Amber went to him. He had the gentlest eyes and a softly dappled grey coat. He nuzzled round her pockets as she stroked him.

"He's lovely," she said.

"We call him Jinks for short," said Lisa.

"What about that one?" said Donna, pointing to a more fine-boned pony at the end of the line.

"He's called Tango," said Lisa. "He's—"

"I'll have him," interrupted Donna. "He's not brilliant but he's the nearest to Sparkle, my thoroughbred pony. He'll have to do."

Amber groaned. Donna was so embarrassing. It was going to be more difficult than she'd thought to keep her promise to herself.

Lisa was unmoved. "I'll be riding Tango," she said firmly. "He's just a baby."

"I can handle him," said Donna.

"I'm sure you could," agreed Lisa. "But he's so new to the trails he gets excited easily.

Now, let's go over the preparation routine, shall we? The sooner we get up into the hills the better, I'd say!"

"Is anyone else coming?" asked Amber, as Lisa brought out brushes and hoofpicks.

Lisa shook her head. "There were going to be more," she said, "but they cancelled at the last minute. Double-booked with a show or something."

She explained about grooming and tacking up, with frequent interruptions from Donna who kept saying they knew all that.

Lisa continued patiently. Good thing too, thought Amber, because they didn't know about keeping the head collar on under the bridle so that it was always there when you needed to tie up your pony. "Just knot the lead ropes round the ponies' necks," said Lisa.

Then she showed them how to put the panniers under the saddle but on top of the numnah. Finally they learnt how to make their waterproofs into a long thin roll and tie them in front of the saddle. "Let's hope we won't need them!" said Lisa.

At last, it was time to mount.

"I'm so excited!" said Molly. "I'm sure I'll be all right on Clover."

Amber smiled. She'd taken a liking to Jinks. But Donna had complained so much all the time they were getting ready that Amber had offered to change ponies. Only to be flatly turned down. "Why would I want him?" said Donna. "He's just as awful as this stupid animal."

"Don't listen," Amber whispered in Jinks's ear, as they set off up the steep hill.

Amber was surprised how quickly they left the lane behind and were riding along gritty paths on open moorland.

You could see for miles across vast stretches of heather to rolling hills on every side. It was breathtaking. So different from the bridlepaths at home which, though lovely, didn't have such spectacular views. Jinks stepped out purposefully. Lisa told them about travelling over long distances, how the ponies needed to be able to stretch their necks forward. "Just keep a light contact on the mouth with the reins," she said.

"They look like washing lines," grumbled Donna. "That's what Jen would say."

Soon they trotted and then cantered up a wide grassy track. Donna took the lead.

"Wait at the top!" called Lisa.

Descending into the valley on the other side of the hill, Donna pushed Gus in front again.

"You can lead if you like," said Lisa. "Gus enjoys being in front, but take it steady. There's no hurry."

They all knew how to lean back when going downhill but it felt really strange on such a steep slope. They had to lock their knees so that their legs were absolutely straight. They'd never had to keep it up for so long.

"I don't like it," said Molly.

"You're doing fine," said Lisa. "Just go with Clover's rhythm. He'll look after you."

Tango, on the other hand, was dancing about. Sort of side-stepping down the hill, Amber thought, almost skipping. Lisa certainly had her hands full.

Once they were down in the valley, they stopped for lunch. There was a stream where all the ponies were keen to drink and a fence nearby to tether them.

Amber sank onto a grassy bank with her lunch pack. "This is fantastic!" she said. "I've always wanted to picnic with a pony!"

"We might come across a herd of wild ponies this afternoon," said Lisa.

"I've seen wild ponies on Exmoor," said Donna. "I got really close. I even persuaded one of them to eat out of my hand!"

Amber caught Molly's eye and tried not to giggle.

They heard a good deal more about Donna's exploits with wild ponies before it was time to move on.

"Check your girths," said Lisa, mounting Tango. "Everyone ready?"

They climbed steadily around the contours of the next hill, one behind the other, Donna still in the lead.

"Look!" said Lisa, as they reached the other side. "There they are!"

A herd of ponies was grazing peacefully close to a small lake far below them.

"See the stallion!" said Lisa. "The white one standing a little apart from the others."

"Let's get nearer!" cried Donna, setting off on a downward track.

"No. Wait!" called Lisa. "It gets very boggy in places."

"I'll be careful!" Donna shouted back.

"Donna!" yelled Lisa.

But Donna took no notice.

She careered headlong down the slope. Amber could see she had no intention of being wary. She was getting closer and closer to the lake. On the far side, the wild ponies lifted their heads.

Suddenly Gus stopped. Donna urged him on. Gus refused to move. Donna kicked him angrily. In answer, Gus put down his head, tipped up his rear and sent Donna flying.

What happened next took place so quickly, Amber could hardly take it in. One minute Donna was in the air. The next she had landed and was swallowed up in thick black sludge. Only her arms and head were visible.

"Don't struggle!" shouted Lisa, riding swiftly down the path. She jumped off Tango and knotted Gus and Tango's lead ropes together. "Keep as still as you can!"

But Donna was flailing her arms about.

"I'm sinking!" she screamed.

"No, you're not," said Lisa. "I'm going to

throw you a rope and pull you out."

But Lisa couldn't throw the rope and control the ponies at the same time. Though Gus was patiently standing by, Tango was frantically pulling backwards on his reins which were looped over Lisa's arm. She tried to calm him but he kept jerking away, snorting in fright.

Amber leapt off Jinks, thrust the reins into Molly's hands, and ran to join them.

"I'll take Tango," she said.

"Thanks," said Lisa. She threw the rope well but Donna only made a half-hearted attempt to catch it. Her screaming had died to a terrified sobbing. "I can't, I can't."

"You must try!" cried Lisa.

Again she threw the rope. This time it landed right in front of Donna.

"Grab it!" shouted Amber.

Donna put out her hand. "I can't."

"Go on!" yelled Amber. "You're nearly there."

Donna reached forward – and grasped it.

"Now hang on!" yelled Lisa. She began to heave on the rope. It took seconds to realize no amount of pulling would have any effect.

"Shall I help pull?" said Amber.

"No," said Lisa. "Can you hold Gus for me as well as Tango?"

"I think so," said Amber.

"Don't let go, Donna!" said Lisa. "We'll soon have you free!"

Quickly she turned Gus round, undid his reins, and tied one end to the rope and the other round the saddle.

"Now lead Gus forward, Amber. Gently," she warned.

Gus took a step, felt Donna's weight behind him and faltered.

"Come on! Please, please!" begged Amber.

Gus tried again. This time he surged forward, almost knocking Amber over in his effort.

Slowly, with a great sucking noise, Donna came out of the bog.

"Gus, you're a hero!" Amber whispered in his ear.

They were all quiet as they resumed their journey. Amber felt desperately sorry for Donna. Her clothes stank, she was covered in slime and, worst of all, Lisa put her on a lead rein all the way to the farmhouse where they were spending the night.

Only once did Donna say something. "How was I to know there was a bog?"

No one answered.

Later, when they were all clean and fed, Lisa took Donna to one side.

"And there's an end to it," she said, when they came back. "Tomorrow it's best hoof forward and heigh-ho for wild camping!"

The wild campsite turned out to be everything Amber had ever dreamed of and more ... miles from anywhere and right next to the sea! A field with a backdrop of pine woods, a stone wall around it and two gates: one through which they passed on their descent and one by the sea through which, Lisa promised them, they would go as soon as they'd unloaded their gear from the ponies.

"Are we going to ride along the beach?" asked Amber. "Can we canter?"

Lisa agreed. "But take it steady," she warned. "It's not a race!"

No one looked at Donna but they all knew who Lisa was directing her comments towards.

Although they'd travelled all day in the hills, the ponies perked up when they made their way down a gently sloping path to the sea. They were eager to go.

But Donna held Gus back. "I don't think I'll risk it," she said. "It doesn't look safe."

Lisa drew in her breath sharply. "The sand's quite firm," she said.

Amber felt sorry for Donna until she noticed the smirk on her face. As the ponies bounded forwards, Donna was right there with them, urging Gus on. She didn't appear to be in the least bit frightened.

It was such a different sensation riding on a flat surface after, for the most part, rough tracks and trails. The ponies loved the change of speed. Amber wanted it to last for ever.

On their return, they cantered through

the shallows. Fine spray spurted up around them. It felt like flying through fountains, thought Amber. Donna, at her side, was keeping pace, leaning forward in the saddle, laughing.

Even Molly was enthusiastic. "Clover really enjoyed it!" she said when they slowed their ponies to a walk, "and he stopped as soon as I asked him!"

Lisa opened the gate for them and made sure it was closed after they'd all gone through. "We'll feed the ponies," she said, "and then we'll put up the tents. We've brought two so either you can all squash up into one or maybe someone would care to join me?"

There was a moment's awkward silence.

"I'd like to," said Molly. "If that's all right."

"Thanks a lot," muttered Amber, under cover of removing saddles and bridles.

"Well, Donna wasn't going to offer, was

she?" whispered Molly. "I felt sorry for Lisa."

"I feel sorry for me!" said Amber.

Donna made no effort at all when she and Amber were given their tent to assemble. It was left entirely to Amber to sort out what slotted into where but at last it was done. There was plenty of room for two. Amber, remembering her promise, chattered away pleasantly as they unpacked the few things they had been able to bring. But Donna hardly answered.

"Are you all right?" said Amber eventually. Perhaps Donna wasn't feeling well or something.

"Fine," snapped Donna.

Amber gave up. She stepped outside the tent. The air was still, not even a murmur of a breeze. The sky, slashed with pink, gave promise of heat for the following day. Out to sea there was some kind of boat making its slow journey across the horizon. Close to shore was a tiny island.

Delicious smells drifted across from the direction of the other tent. Amber hurried over, suddenly realizing she was very, very hungry.

They dined on pasta, vegetables and tomato sauce, none of which was to Donna's liking. "It's not a proper meal," she complained. "It's just out of packets." She declined the dried fruit and nuts that followed. "I don't eat rabbit food," she said.

After the meal they washed up in a clear stream at the edge of the field. Then Lisa suggested a walk or a game. "Or do you just want to turn in?" she asked. "It's been a long day."

Donna decided to go for a walk.

"That's OK," said Lisa. "Half an hour all right?"

Donna nodded and went off down the field. Lisa and Molly settled to a game of mini-draughts and Amber brought out her diary. She began to write up the day's events but she felt restless. She wandered up the field to chat to Jinks. He wasn't really interested but seemed happy to let Amber stand with her arm draped over his neck.

Amber could see Donna down on the beach. She walked for a few paces, stopped, then carried on. Amber wondered why. It was only when Donna turned that Amber saw she was holding a phone. So that's why she'd taken herself off ... well, it was understandable. She'd tried to get in touch with her mother the evening before but hadn't been able to. It didn't look as if she was having much success tonight either.

"Couldn't you get a signal?" said Amber later, in their tent.

"What's it to you?" said Donna.

"I was only asking," said Amber. Hopeless. No one could say she hadn't tried to be friendly, but if Donna was going to snap every time she spoke to her…

"She wasn't there," said Donna suddenly. "They must have gone away."

Amber assumed Donna meant her parents.

"Have they got a mobile you could try?" she suggested.

"Switched off," said Donna. "They never said they were going anywhere." She flounced into her sleeping bag.

Amber wriggled gratefully into hers. She couldn't imagine her parents going away without saying anything. She snuggled down and fell asleep dreaming of hills, sky, sea and a certain dapple grey pony, the colour of sunlight and shadows.

Amber was first up in the morning. She eased herself out of the tent and stood, yawning. It was a lovely day, already warm. She looked over at the ponies. Gus and

Clover were grazing together at the top of the field. But Jinks and Tango were nowhere to be seen.

Quickly, Amber scanned the whole field, then ran all round it, thinking perhaps the missing ponies were in a dip in one of the corners where she couldn't see. It was then she noticed that the bottom gate was open. Amber raced down to the beach.

It was deserted.

"Over there!" a voice called from behind her. Amber turned round. Donna, Molly and Lisa were pointing out to sea. Amber looked. Sure enough, there were two dark shapes on the tiny island.

"How can they be ours?" asked Amber when she got back to camp.

"They'd swim across," said Lisa. "What I'd like to know is how they got out of the field in the first place. I'm sure I closed the gate last night."

Amber avoided catching Donna's eye,

hoping she'd say something. It must have been Donna. She was the only one who'd gone down to the beach later on.

No one spoke.

"Well, I'll just have to go and get them," said Lisa.

"How?" said Molly.

"Swim!" said Lisa. "Don't worry. At least I can ride one of them back."

"Oh," breathed Amber, "how amazing! Can I help?"

Lisa shook her head. "What you can do if you want to be really helpful is start the breakfast. I'm going to need it!"

Donna went back inside her tent. Amber and Molly began to assemble the stove and the pans but Amber kept leaping up to watch Lisa's progress.

"Where is she now?" said Molly, turning the sausages.

"Just reached the island!" cried Amber.

Molly added bacon to the pan. Amber

found butter, tiny portions of jam, and bananas. "It's going to be a huge breakfast!" she said.

"Have another look," said Molly, keeping her eye on the bacon.

Amber jumped up. "She's on Jinks, I think," she reported. "Imagine riding bareback on a horse that's swimming!"

"I can't find the bread rolls," said Molly. "I was sure we had some."

"They're in our tent," said Amber, and she ran to fetch them.

As she reached the tent, she heard Donna's voice. Amber paused at the entrance. She knew she shouldn't. Mum always said, "No eavesdropper ever heard any good about themselves."

But Donna wasn't talking about her.

"Lisa's useless," Donna was saying. "She's not fit to be in charge. She's lost two ponies because she left a gate open and now they've swum off to an island. She let me ride straight into a bog on the first day, didn't warn me or anything, and I nearly suffocated. And yesterday she made us ride along a beach with quicksand!"

Amber gasped.

It was all lies.

Every word.

For a moment Amber stood, unable to move. Then she dashed into the tent, grabbed the packet of bread rolls and ran back to Molly. Her thoughts raced. Donna must have got through to her mother. But why all the lies? It was so unfair. Lisa had looked after them really well, especially Donna. If it hadn't been for her, Donna could easily have been buried alive. Amber shuddered.

"Thanks," said Molly. "Lisa's nearly back."

Amber flew down the field to open the gate.

"Are you all right?" she asked, as Lisa rode through.

"Luckily," said Lisa. "Although it's not something I'd want to do again." Despite the warmth of the day, she couldn't stop shivering. "I'm more than ready for breakfast!"

The meal went smoothly, except for Donna hissing in Amber's ear as she sat down, "Snooping again? Why can't you mind your own business?"

Lisa didn't even mention the unnecessary journey she'd just had to make. Amber marvelled at her calm.

After breakfast, when she and Molly went to wash up, Amber told her about the conversation she'd overheard.

Molly was outraged. "That's horrible!" she said. "It was Donna's fault, not Lisa's."

"Catch Donna admitting that!" said Amber.

Before they left, Lisa spread out some maps on the grass.

"You might like to find your own route today," she suggested.

Donna looked pointedly out to sea.

The maps were arranged in sequence, each in a plastic case attached to a string which they could hang round their necks. Lisa gave them out. "Yours is first, Molly!"

Molly studied the highlighted line in front of her. "On the beach?" she offered hesitantly.

"Correct!" said Lisa.

It was sad to leave their campsite, thought Amber as they moved off, but fun to ride through the waves again, taking their time, letting the ponies get into their stride. Who knew what wonders lay ahead?

Molly guided them up into the hills through dense woodland. The path was steep and the trees grew so tall and close together, not a slant of sunlight pierced through. As they came out onto a moor, they felt dazzled by the brightness.

They paused to look back. Way below they could see their field and the beach and the sea shimmering into the distance.

Amber sighed.

"If we did an award when we're older, could we come back here?" she asked.

Lisa nodded. "Around here anyway. Do you think you'll have a go, then?"

"Definitely," said Amber.

Molly was keen too. "Especially if I rode Clover!" she said.

"And you, Donna?" said Lisa.

The question hung in the air. The answer, when it came, was like a whiplash. "I hate it!" said Donna. "If you must know, I hate your whole stupid trip!"

Lisa didn't flinch. "I'm sorry you feel like that," she said quietly. "Can you say why?"

Donna shrugged.

"You do like riding?" prompted Lisa. "Well, you must I suppose—"

"I like riding Sparkle," interrupted Donna.

"I like showing and jumping. But not this endless mooching on. It's boring."

"I see," said Lisa. "Well, let's try to make today more fun for you. It's your map next if you'd like to have a go."

"No, thanks," said Donna. She wrenched the map from around her neck. "No point, is there? I'm never doing this again."

Lisa took the map and turned Tango inland. "That's a shame," she said.

Amber strove to put Donna out of her mind and give herself up to the joyful rhythm of Jinks. The sun was shining and they had a whole day's riding ahead of them.

They stopped for lunch on the moor but not for long. Suddenly, the weather had changed. Black clouds rolled up with alarming swiftness.

"It can do this in the mountains," said Lisa. "We'd better put waterproofs on before we leave."

No sooner had they done so than grumbles of thunder were heard and the first stinging drops of rain fell.

"Your turn to guide us, Amber!"

Amber studied her map, brushing the rain off its plastic case.

"Downhill next," she decided. "Then it looks like we cross a river!"

"Oh dear," said Molly.

"Is it deep?" asked Amber. "Will the ponies swim?"

"I hope not!" said Lisa.

But the river was deep enough to warrant the riders lifting their feet well up. The ponies waded across happily, except Tango who was in the lead, fretting a little and leaping onto the opposite bank sooner than was necessary. Amber was glad Jinks was well-behaved.

"Now we go along a lane," said Amber, "through a village, then more lanes." It didn't sound very exciting. But it turned out to be fun, Jinks being easily the best at trotting uphill, overtaking everyone, much to Donna's annoyance.

When they came onto moorland again they cantered, but the grass was becoming quite slippery in the rain.

"We'll stick to the tracks, I think," said Lisa.

Amber picked up the trail when they reached the edge of the moor and began their descent. "It looks very wiggly!" she said.

"We'll take it steady," said Lisa. "Single file! I'll go first, then you Donna, then Amber. Molly, you're our rearguard!"

The path zigzagged down the hillside, steep and narrow, hardly visible to the riders as it was so overgrown with bracken. Further down, the land became almost bare with outcrops of rock.

Lisa paused to see if everyone was all right.

"I'll be glad to get to the bottom!" called Molly.

"Me too!" said Amber. Her whole body ached from leaning back.

"Not far now," said Lisa, carrying on. But suddenly she stopped so abruptly that the ponies clattered into each other.

"What is it?" cried Molly.

"I don't know," said Amber. But she could hear a low rumbling.

"A landslide!" yelled Donna.

Immediately came Lisa's voice sounding angry. "It's nothing of the kind," she said. "It's just a bit of scree."

Amber knew about scree, small stones covering a hillside. She stood up in her stirrups. The rain had loosened it, showering it down the slope.

Lisa urged Tango forward but he spun round. She tried again but once more he swung backwards. "He's just a bit unnerved," said Lisa. "He doesn't like the noise."

Or the rain, thought Amber, or the stones bouncing about. Who could blame him? But Lisa knew what she was doing. Taking her time, she calmed him, spoke to him gently...

"Oh, for goodness sake!" burst out Donna impatiently. "I'll go first."

But there was no room for two ponies side by side on such a path. As Donna pushed past on Gus, Tango lost his footing and fell.

At first horse and rider seemed caught up in a wild tangle as they tumbled down the hillside but as Amber watched, horrified, they separated. Tango landed, rolled over and stood up.

But Lisa gave no sign of movement. She lay where she had fallen.

"We have to get down there!" screamed Amber. "Go on, Donna!"

"I can't," whispered Donna.

"Please," begged Amber. "You have to go first. Take your time and follow the path."

Slowly, Donna rode on. It seemed an age to Amber before all three of them were safely at the bottom of the hill. She jumped off Jinks and knelt beside Lisa.

"There's a pulse," said Amber, "and she's still breathing." But though she said Lisa's name out loud, there was no response.

"What are we going to do?" whispered Molly, who was trying to hold the ponies.

"Get help," said Amber. She stood up, pulled her phone out of her pocket and dialled 999. Her fingers trembled. Twice she tried. Then she realized. No signal. Perhaps it was because they were in a valley.

She tried to remember what Dad had taught her about survival. She couldn't think.

"What shall I do?" said Donna. Her face was ashen. She had dismounted and was holding both Gus and Tango. "This is all my fault. I'm so sorry."

"We mustn't move Lisa and we need to keep her warm," said Amber.

"Sleeping bags?" suggested Donna. She set to work on the panniers.

Molly took over all four ponies but Amber reached for Jinks and mounted.

"What are you doing?" cried Molly.

"Going back up the hill," said Amber.

Molly stared. "You can't!" Scree littered the path and was still skittering down the slope.

"Higher up there might be a signal," said Amber.

"Why not walk?" said Molly. Amber had thought of that but she knew Jinks would be quicker. If only he didn't slip…

As she set off, Tango whinnied. Jinks hesitated but Amber pressed her heels firmly into his sides and he moved obediently forwards. Though he skidded more than once as they climbed upward, Amber kept him going. As soon as she judged she was high enough, she halted and tried her phone. This time she heard the dialling tone; the line clicked; a voice spoke.

"Emergency rescue," said Amber in response. Quickly she gave the details of the fall.

"Can you give us some idea of where you are?" said the voice.

Amber checked her map and found that her hands were shaking.

"Are you still there?" said the voice. "Can you tell me—"

"Yes," said Amber. She forced her fingers to work.

Slowly and clearly she began to read, finishing with the six numbers of the grid reference: their exact location.

As Amber rode back down the valley, she found that not only were her legs shaking, her whole body felt wobbly. She made herself concentrate on keeping Jinks safely on the path.

When she reached the bottom, she jumped off. Molly was holding the ponies. Donna was kneeling beside Lisa.

"She's so still," whispered Donna. "Are you sure...?"

Amber checked. Lisa was breathing steadily.

"Is someone coming?" said Molly. "Will they be long?"

"They're sending a helicopter," said Amber. There was enough space around them for it to land, she thought, but the noise would be terrifying.

"We have to move the ponies before the rescue team gets here," she decided. "Can you do that?" she asked Molly and Donna. "I'll stay with Lisa."

She tried to remember what she knew about first aid. The most important rule was not to move the injured person but if Lisa regained consciousness, Amber would have to put her in the recovery position so that she didn't choke. What if that did more harm than good? There was no bleeding that she could see, thank goodness, but Lisa's right arm was twisted underneath her. Amber didn't want to make it worse.

She looked up. Molly and Donna had gone well away with the ponies.

There was no sign of a helicopter.

Amber settled herself down. It was no

use worrying about what to do if and when. She took Lisa's hand and told her all about the mad scramble up the hillside and how wonderful Jinks had been. Suddenly she found herself close to tears. She knew Lisa couldn't hear her. But she kept talking. "Help is definitely on the way," said Amber, "so don't you think it isn't."

She tucked the sleeping bags in more closely – and heard a distant murmuring in the sky.

The helicopter was coming!

Amber stood up and waved. Whether it did any good or not, she didn't know, but slowly, with a deafening whirring of its blades, the helicopter landed.

Two men jumped down and ran over to her. While they checked Lisa, making her comfortable and lifting her gently onto a stretcher, Amber told them all she knew.

"She will be all right, won't she?" Amber asked.

"We'll soon have her in hospital," said one of the rescuers cheerfully. "Now what about you and your friends?"

Amber had been thinking about that. "I've got a map," she said. "I can ride my pony and lead Lisa's back to the trail centre."

"We'll let them know you're on the way," said one of the men. "Good luck – and well done!"

An uneasy silence settled on the valley after the helicopter had whirled off into the distance. Amber was glad when Molly and Donna joined her again with the ponies.

"Are you sure you can find the way?" said Molly as they mounted.

"Shouldn't we wait until someone fetches us?" said Donna. "We don't want to get lost."

Amber shook her head. "I think we should at least start," she said. "The ponies have stood still long enough. We'll all feel better on the move."

Amber guided them out of the valley and up into the hills again. They rode along a high ridge and then down into a village, along winding lanes and eventually up onto moorland again. Tango danced along at Amber's side. Jinks stepped out, taking no notice of Tango's antics.

On the moor, Amber found it was harder to follow the route. All the grassy paths looked the same. But when they reached the old drovers' roads, she felt more confident. "We should be able to see the trail centre soon," she said, stopping to check her map.

"There it is!" shouted Molly. "We're almost there."

It was a slow descent down the steep lane. A crowd was waiting at the bottom.

"We sent someone to help you," said one of the staff. "But you'd gone back up into the hills by then. You must be exhausted."

Eager hands reached forward to take the ponies.

"Can I do it?" asked Amber, dismounting. Suddenly she realized she had to say goodbye to Jinks. She wanted to settle him herself.

"I'm so proud of you," said a voice. Amber turned. Her father moved forward and hugged her. "I've heard all about your survival skills!"

"But what are you doing here?" asked Amber as they went to the stable.

"Donna's mother phoned," said Dad. "She's up in Scotland, in some castle or other. Their flight home was delayed so she asked me to fetch you."

"That's fantastic," said Amber, handing Dad the saddle and turning to undo Jinks's bridle.

"The hospital just phoned," said Dad.

Amber felt her legs go wobbly again. "Is Lisa all right?"

"She's fine," said Dad, "and demanding to see you!"

*　*　*

At the hospital, Amber found that Lisa had a broken arm and a broken leg. But nothing that wouldn't mend, Lisa assured her.

"What about concussion?" said Amber. "You were unconscious."

"But you knew how to cope," said Lisa. "I can't thank you enough for what you did. And then you found your way back to the centre! I can tell you one thing: if you'd been doing the award for real, you'd have passed with flying colours!" She smiled. "I hope this hasn't put you off? I wouldn't blame you."

"Not likely!" said Amber. She stood up as Molly popped her head around the door, signalling they had to go.

"Tell Jinks I'm looking forward to it!" said Amber. She gave Lisa a hug. "See you next year!"

It's the first day of Pony Camp at Merryfield Hall Riding School. Five whole days of riding! Amber has been looking forward to it for months. But that evening, Amber sees Oscar the pony being bullied by some boys and she hatches a plan to save him!

BY JUNE CREBBIN

If you've enjoyed reading this book,

look out for...

Short novels for fluent readers